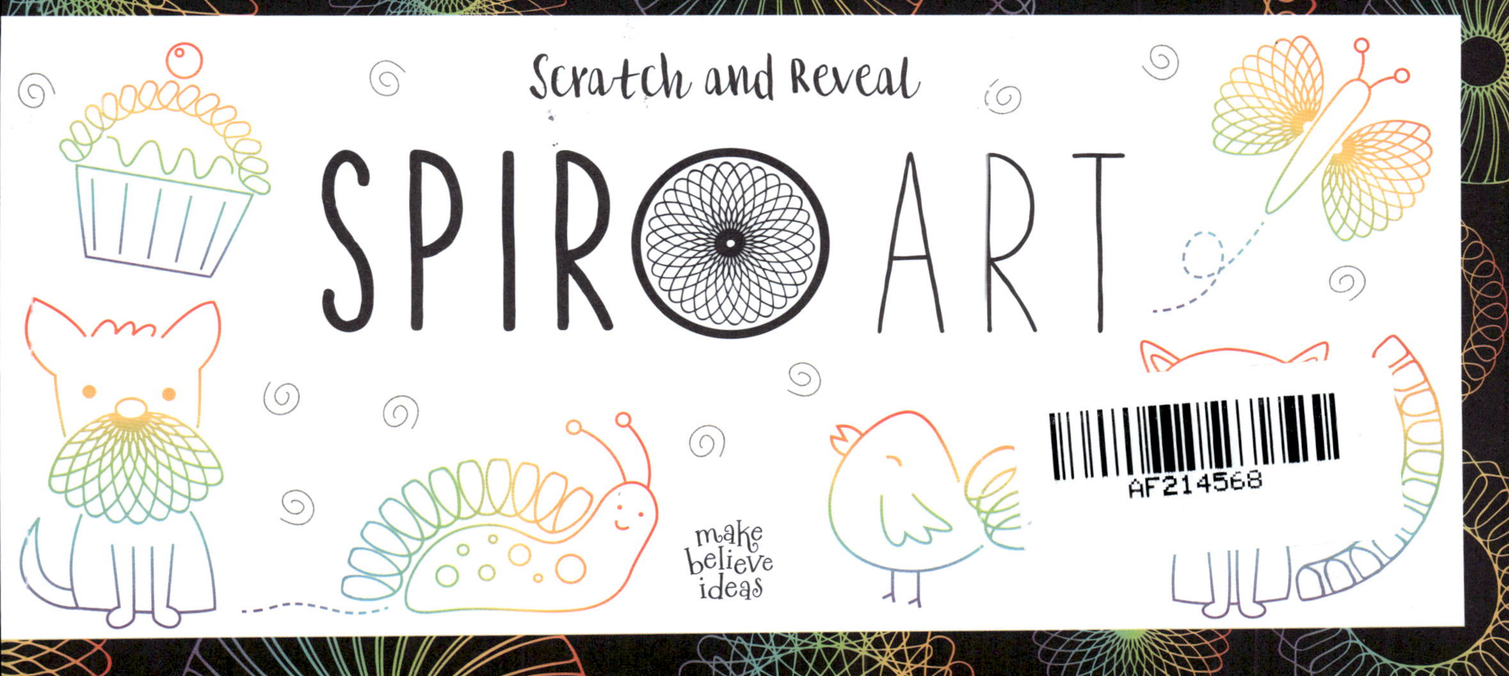

Scratch and Reveal
SPIRO ART
make believe ideas
AF214568

Follow the steps to create stunning spiro art,
and then display it in your press-out picture frame!
Inside this book you will find inspirational ideas
to get you started, and plenty of practice paper.

Here's your Scratch and Reveal toolkit!

1 Position the wheel on the page and hold the frame steady over the top.

2 Place the tip of your pencil or scratcher in one of the shapes on the wheel.

3 Move your pencil or scratcher clockwise around the shape in the wheel.

4 As you draw, the wheel will move around the frame and the spiral will appear.

5 You can use the extra stencil shapes and ruler on your frame to finish your pictures. You can also add your own freehand drawings!

6 Scratching produces a fine black dust. Minimize mess by placing your sheet on an old magazine or newspaper. Your scratcher sharpens just like a pencil.

BLUE WHEEL

Use the diagram to see the spiral patterns you can create with the blue wheel.

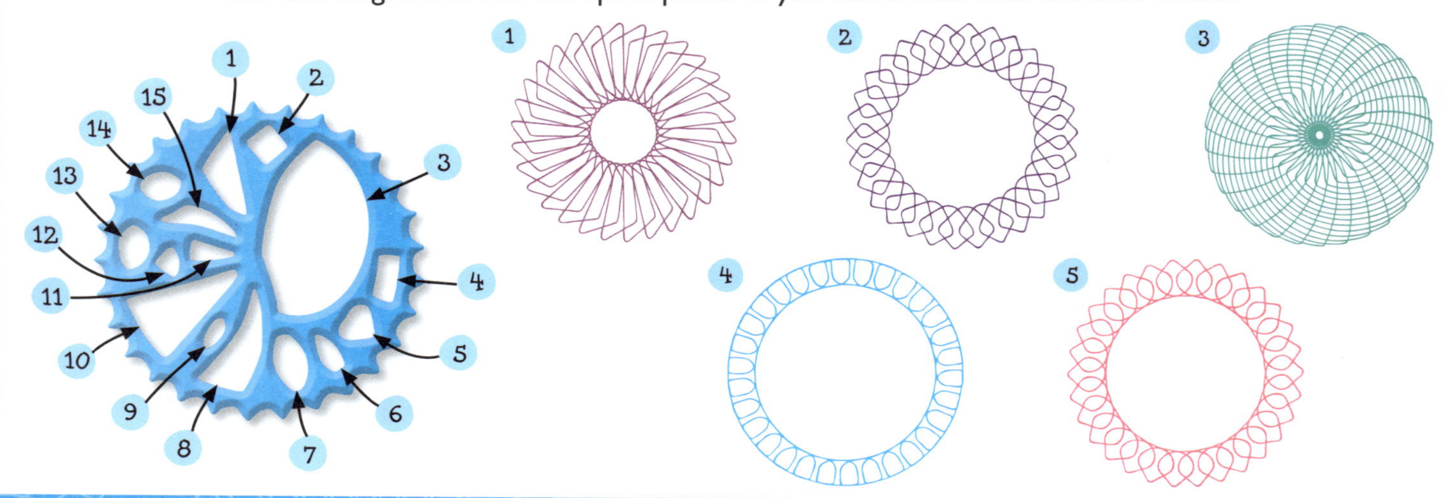

BLUE WHEEL

More spiral patterns you can create with the blue wheel.

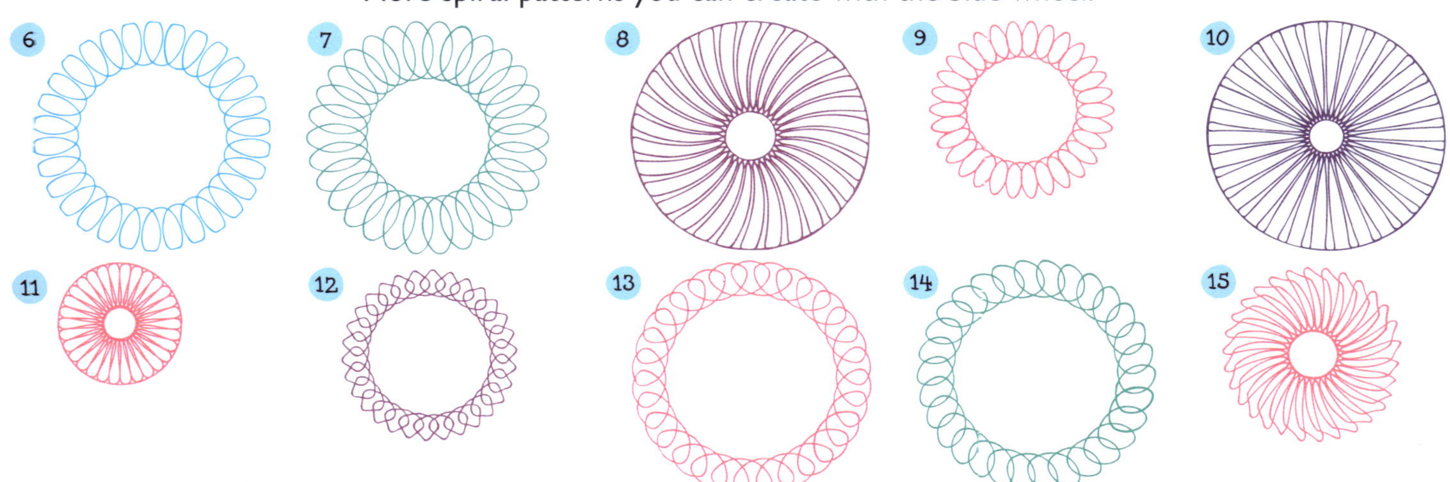

Use the diagram to see the spiral patterns you can create with the green wheel.

More spiral patterns you can create with the green wheel.

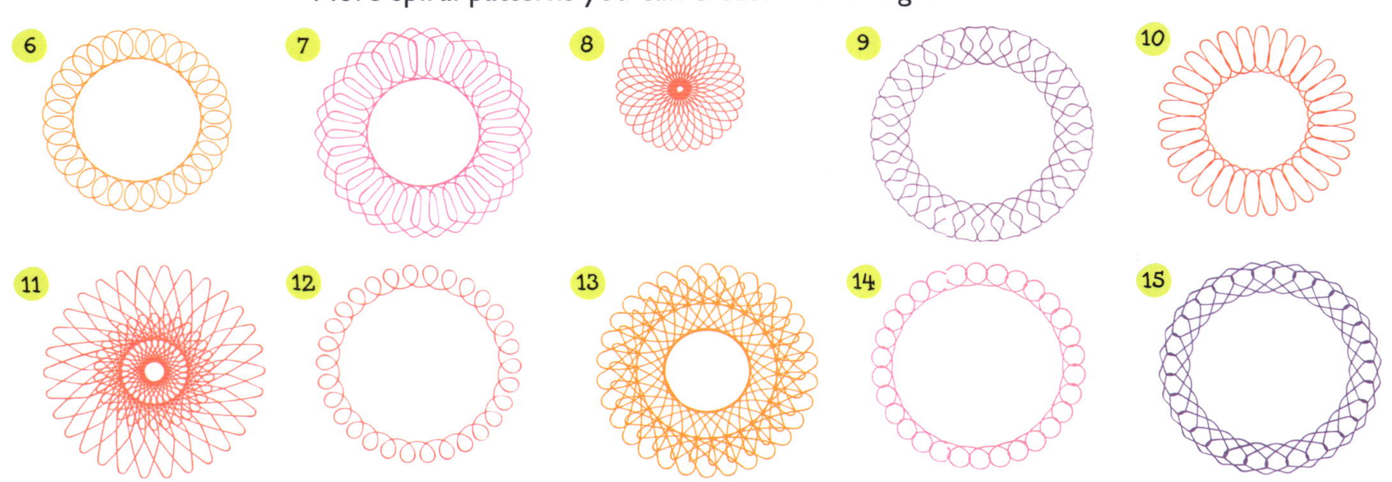

1 Spiraling is easy, but always practice with a pencil and paper first to make sure you know how your design will turn out.

2 The colored numbers next to the spirals tell you which wheel and shape to use to create each spiral.

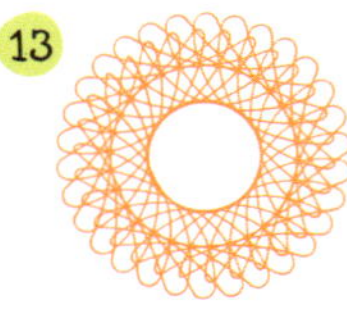

Green wheel
shape 13

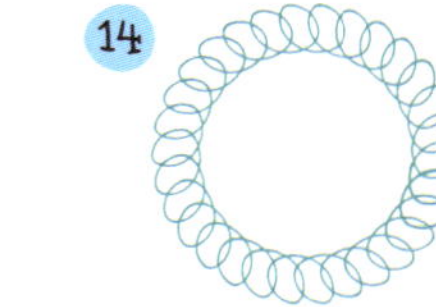

Blue wheel
shape 14

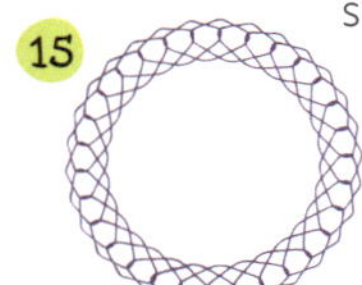

Green wheel
shape 15

3 Some of the pictures on the inspiration pages use just part of a spiral. Practicing first will mean you know where to start and stop, ensuring the shape you scratch is in the right place!

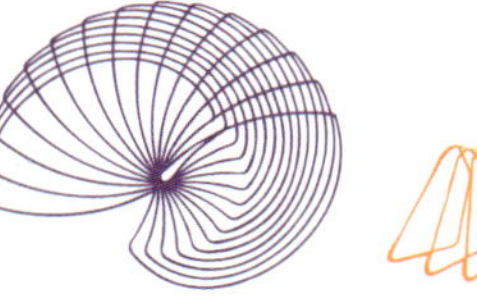

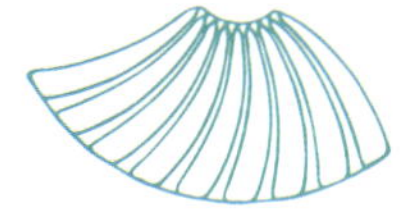

You can use the press-out stencils inside the picture frame to add decorations to your artwork.

1 Find the two stencils in the picture frame, and carefully press them out. You can use the pressed-out pieces to decorate the frame, or draw around them to add more shapes to your artwork.

2 Hold the stencil firmly around the edge to avoid it slipping. Put your scratcher inside the stencil and start scratching an outline. You can scratch all of the shape if you want a block of color.

stencil 1

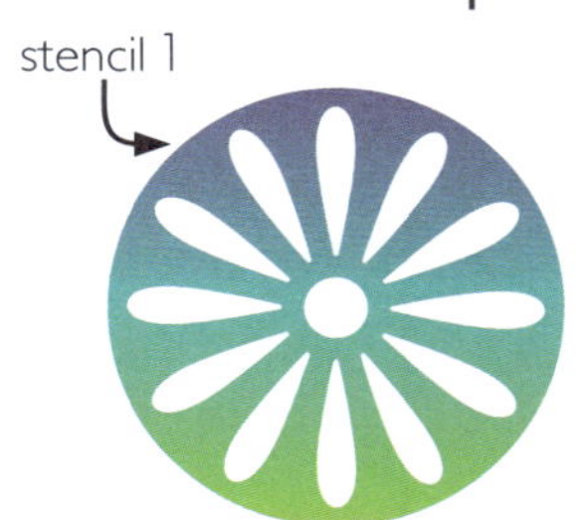

Decorations you can make with stencil 1:

stencil 2

Decorations you can make with stencil 2:

Try rotating the stencil to overlap the shapes.

INSPIRATIONAL IDEAS

11
1
9
8
8
6
Use these pages to give you ideas for sparkly and rainbow spiro scenes.

UP, UP, AND AWAY
8
3
9
8
10

FANCY FLOWERS
10
11
11
3
9
7

WHIRLING WHEELS

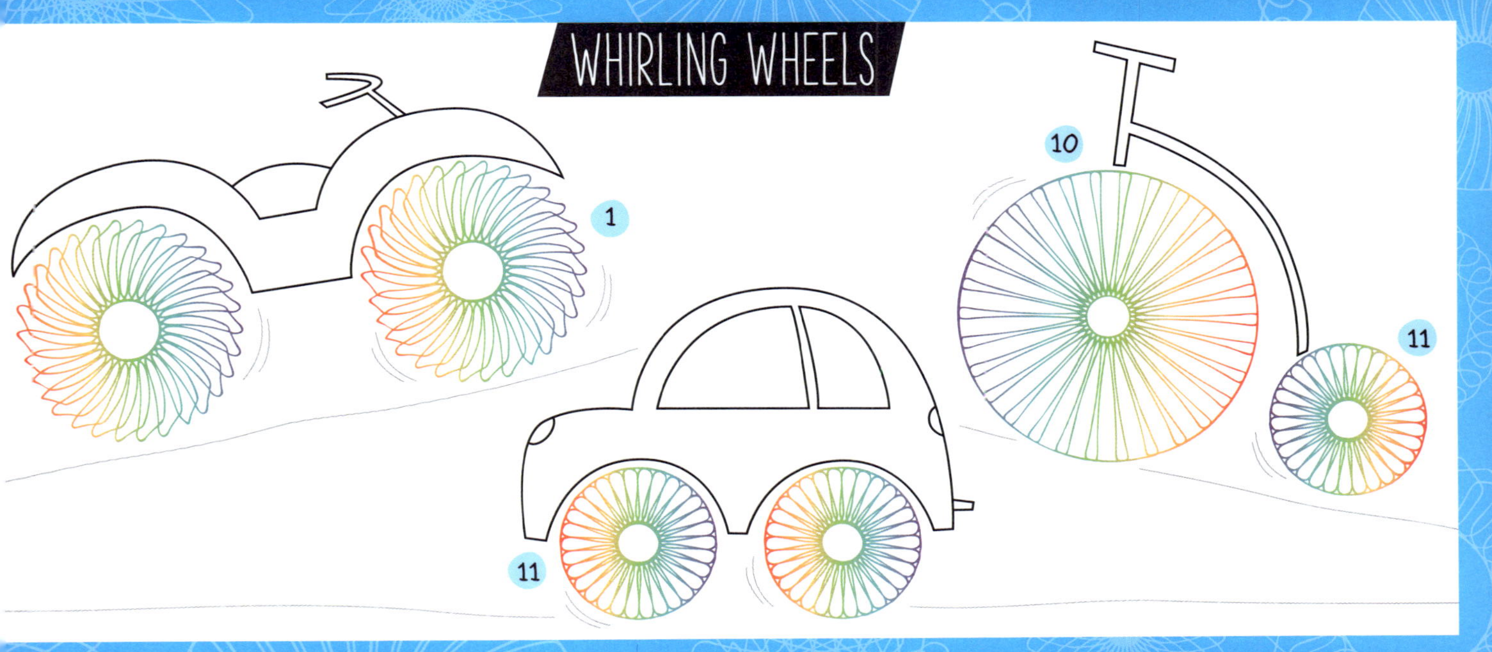

FANTASTIC FIREWORKS
4
8
11
13

SPIRO SKIRTS

PERFECT PETS
4
8
9
8
11
4

SNACK ATTACK
10
15
13
5
1
4

BUGS AND BEASTIES

FABULOUS FAIRIES
11
8

ALIEN ALERT

SALON STYLES

CUTE CREATURES
11
6
1
12
1
12

MIND-BOGGLING BIRDS

UNDER THE SEA
8
8
10
11
2
3
11

BEAUTIFUL BUTTERFLIES
12
7
14
11
8
11

Try out the spiros with an ordinary pencil first.
You can use these pages to practice your picture ideas.